EMISSARY OF BLOOD

CONNOR WHITELEY

EMISSARY OF BLOOD

No part of this book may be reproduced in any form or by any electronic or mechanical means. Including information storage, and retrieval systems, without written permission from the author except for the use of brief quotations in a book review.

This book is NOT legal, professional, medical, financial or any type of official advice.

Any questions about the book, rights licensing, or to contact the author, please email connorwhiteley@connorwhiteley.net

Copyright © 2021 CONNOR WHITELEY

All rights reserved.

DEDICATION
Thank you to all my readers without you I couldn't do what I love.

EMISSARY OF BLOOD

The last of my Guard slammed the immense black iron door behind us as we gracefully marched into the meeting chamber.

I rolled my eyes in disgust.

It was typical of the Emissary of Sanguis to be late.

I suppose it gave me a chance to get the layout of the chamber in case I needed to escape.

A small smile flashed on my face as I remembered the crazy situations I got myself into during my military service.

Thankfully, I was rather adept at escape.

With a flick of my smooth white-gloved hands, I ordered my Guard to stand firmly at the edges of the circular chamber.

Their thick metal armoured boots echoed around the chamber as they stomped over to their position.

Additionally, their pitch-black armour provided a chilling contrast against the blood-red walls with their stone carvings of life-size skulls of laughing horned humans.

More chills ran down my spine.

Stepping forward, my white armoured boots chipped the golden marble floor slightly. Whilst I made my way over to the giant black granite table in front.

It looked beautiful and shiny, so I ran my long fingers across it.

The cold smooth stone felt pleasant.

Then I shot them back.

Two of my fingers were sliced deep.

Red blood flowing out from them.

Then they healed.

Looking at the table, I saw my blood was gone.

My eyebrows rose.

A part of me wanting to shout or find the nearest Sanguisian and get answers. Yet I am an Ambassador for the mighty nation of Insenguard. My Country could burn Sanguis with a single thought, but the Empress seemed interested in Sanguis. Therefore, I must do my duty.

I wandered over to the far edge of the meeting chamber, clocking a rather beautiful diamond chandelier with gold flecks on the ceiling.

When I got to the edge of the meeting chamber, I looked out a large crystal window. To see great caves ripped into the earth and mighty glowing veins of gold, bronze and diamonds.

Presumably, before the Sanguisian ripped it out of the earth.

Maybe this was the Empress' interest in Sanguis?

I coughed as I faintly smelt rotting flesh.

My Guards walked towards me.

Their mighty golden spears ready to strike.

I waved them back.

With a cough, I ready myself.

Yet the smell of rotting flesh and blood still lingered.

The iron door thundered open.

I spun around.

Reaching for a gun that was not there.

I forced my military instincts to die.

My Guard tensed.

Thick blue smoke rolled into the chamber.

Three figures stepped out.

My Guard were preparing to strike.

I waved my hand elegantly to stop them.

They snapped to attention.

Glaring at the three figures, I saw the two figures walking behind the third figure, where long slender white beings. Their skin ghostly white and their faces were cold, distant.

I tried to look them in the eye, but their eyes were glassy.

My eyes scanned their slim bodies to see only malnourished bones dressed in paper thin iron armour.

Although, a great coldness pulsed through me.

Some within Insenguard took it as a signal from the God Empress. I don't know what I believe, but I trust in my Empress.

I needed to be careful.

Shifting my focus to the central figure walking towards me, I saw an extremely tall woman. Maybe three metres tall with a ten-inch waist that her night-black dress stuck tightly.

Her movements were angelic and measured.

The more I looked at her, the more my skin itched.

I almost felt as if beetles were crawling over me.

I dismissed the thought.

Looking at her face, a chill ran down my spine as I saw her sharp-pointed chin and slender face.

When she opened her mouth to speak, the air crackled with magical energy. Before her snarling words bellowed in the chamber.

"So, you, you come to see us. The Mighty Dead warriors of old have returned, returned," she said as she ran her long black nails across the granite table.

I composed myself.

"Yes, mighty Emissary. Insenguard was reconquered and we have reclaimed our homeland. Now, I must…"

She etched a symbol into the granite table.

Her nails screamed as they cut the granite.

My ears bleed slightly.

I looked at the symbol.

A part of me wanted to gasp in awe at the beauty of the curves and artistry that went into its swirls and twirls.

However, apart of me commanded me to run and hide, or call for reinforcements.

Just another military instinct overreacting, I'm sure.

"What is this Symbol, my dear Emissary? Insenguard has no knowledge of this,"

In all honesty, I did not want to play any political games. I hate this place and I would have preferred to accept the Empress' offer of armed legionnaires outside.

But I have a job to do, regardless of my feelings.

The Emissary gave a devilish smile.

"This is the symbol of Death, Death in our Culture, culture. You Insenguardians invaded our land and now some amongst us want to mark you,"

"Insenguard did no such thing, my dear Emissary. We were running an operation to protect this dimension against demons. I must extend my deepest apologies for stepping onto your sacred Blood Grounds,"

She gave a mocking bow.

"Well, well, at least you have, have apologised. That is something, Unbloodied. I must confess, confess there is a majority within our ranks, ranks that sees this as an opportunity, opportunity,"

She opened the door to peace.

I took it.

"And mighty Emissary, this is how Insenguard sees this event as well. It is a chance for us to trade and bring peace to this forgotten region of Chituera,"

She cocked her head.

I wished I had magic for these moments. I would have loved to be able to read her mind.

She smiled.

Showing rows upon rows of dagger-like teeth.

My arm went for a gun that wasn't there.

I knew what these creatures were. Some called them humans, but they are nothing like me.

Other call them demons but they are of this world.

I call them Bloodhunters.

I needed to escape, but the Empress sent me here for a reason.

Politely, I smiled at the Emissary and asked: "How about I make a quick call to my Government and I can arrange a gesture of Good Faith before we start negotiations,"

She stared at me.

My heart raced.

"Negative, Ambassador. We are going to talk in my private chambers,"

My Guard snapped into a fighting stance.

All I needed to do was move my hand and they would slaughter these Bloodhunters.

"Stand down and wait outside," I commanded, my voice uncertain.

The Emissary carefully walked over to me.

Her mouth was so close to my ear, I could feel her damp breath.

"If you do not, not come with me, me. My fraction will decimate your, your military escorts on the surface, surface,"

"My Lady?" one of my Guard asked.

With command and authority, I boomed: "Wait outside,"

The Emissary stepped away and grinned.

I nodded to my Guard.

They returned to attention.

The Emissary pointed towards a door that grew out of the wall.

My heart raced.

Sweat poured down my skin.

I walked through the door.

The Emissary close behind me.

***

The Emissary slammed the door shut behind me.

I turned around to face her.

The walls moaned a little as the door was consumed once more by the wall.

My heart quickened.

My breath increased.

This was not normal.

This place was not natural.

I needed to escape.

Yet my duty is to see this through so that is what I shall do in the Empress' name.

My memories of stories arose as I recalled magical tales of witches and demons creating mystic labyrinths to capture their prey.

I was not going to become this creature's prey.

Subtly turning my head side to side, I checked the room for weapons or ways to escape.

I found none.

Instead, all I saw was the blood red domed walls of the room rising to a golden point in the domed ceiling.

I quickly looked at the golden point to see it looked as if it was a bowl of some kind.

Memories of my military days danced across my mind as I remember fighting in pitch-black tunnels a few years ago. I remember the screams of my comrades and the flash of gunfire.

I needed to marshal that courage once again.

Turning my attention to the Emissary, I saw her studying me.

She looked up and down my body. Making

sure she remembered every inch and joint of my soft fleshy body.

I remember a member of the Death Cult of Assassins doing this to me when the Empress ordered us to complete a mission together.

The artful Slaughter of the Assassins still terrified me.

Yet I found out in the bitter end why the Assassin was eyeing me up. That was before she tried to kill me.

The Cult said the assassin was a traitor but her skill still gave me sleepless nights.

If this Emissary was eyeing me up for the same reason then I needed to flee.

I took a careful step forward, my armoured feet chipping the cold lead floor as I stepped.

The Emissary frowned.

I stopped.

I was not going to escape for now.

Then I saw her lips move almost as if she was mouthing unknown words.

A gentle humming filled the air.

Concurrent with the smell of sweat and blood filling my senses.

"Emissary," I spoke.

She stopped.

Her lips turned grey and thin.

The gentle humming stopped.

My heart and muscles relaxed a little.

"Why did you bring me in here, mighty Ally?"

Her mouth turned bitter.

"Do not pretend, pretend Insenguardian scum that we, we are allies,"

Instantly, I was confused.

Why did she want me away from my Guard?

I needed to kill her, but something inside stopped me.

"I apologise but I promise you there can be peace between our cultures,"

She playfully whipped up her claws.

Fear was starting to grip me.

Hopefully, my Guard would sense something was wrong soon.

"Little Ambassador, my government wants peace. My Government wants to sign a treaty,"

"That is excellent, my friend. Together…"

I stopped instantly- alerted to the expression on her face.

She was saying what her government wanted.

She was not saying what she wanted or needed.

This Emissary might have been a part of this culture, but something was very wrong.

Flashes of other Sanguisian appeared in my mind as I realised she was different to them.

Her fellow Sanguisian were kind, hard-working people.

I remember a little boy running up to me as soon as I got here. His body was malnourished and his teeth black.

Yet he still insisted I have a shard of his bread.

Moments later after I turned a few corners, some adults did the same.

These people were about welcoming others.

This Emissary was not.

Stupidly, I snapped a gun that was not there.

I swore under my breath.

I wish I had a gun so I could paint this domed chamber with her brain.

The Emissary took a step closer.

My brain told my body to move back, but it didn't respond.

When the Emissary was a metre away from me, I smelt her earthy perfume with heavy notes of forest and metals.

I wanted to gag on the perfume.

I forced my body to relax.

"Now, now little scum. You, you will not escape. My Government is wrong. My Government shall fall,"

It shattered all illusions of this Emissary.

Her true nature was revealed.

Her right hand turned blood red.

No, heavens no.

Her hand leaked litres of blood onto the floor as blood flowed from her hand in an endless thick river.

My eyes widened.

I ran for the wall.

She flickered her hand.

Dark red blood splashed up my armour.

Hissing filled the air as the blood dissolved my armour.

I ripped it off.

I forced myself against a wall.

Its cold texture chilling me to the bone.

Still the Emissary smiled.

My heart pounded.

My breathing rapidly increased.

The smell of death and corpses filled my senses.

The air crackled loudly with magical energy as the Emissary's lips moved.

Memories of other situations flashed near-death situations popped in my mind.

Reminding me of the terror I've faced.

Immense screaming filled the domed chamber.

The sound of cracking metal filed my senses.

Followed by the sound of shattering bones.

My Guards' screams deafened me.

The emissary waved a hand.

A door opened.

I froze in terror.

The human skulls in the walls crawled out.

Their long humanoid scaly bodies stretching in their newfound freedom.

Their hands revealing metre long talons dripping an endless river of dark rich blood.

Instantly, their talons ripped into the warm flesh of my Guard.

Within seconds, they were slaughtered.

Whatever these abominable creatures where they needed to die.

The Bloodhunters stared at me.

The creatures snarled.

I longed for a weapon.

My body wanted nothing more than to launch myself into these creatures and shatter their supernatural bodies.

The Emissary stared at me.

She smiled.

I knew my fate was sealed.

***

Fear gripped me.

I was deep inside enemy territory without a weapon.

It was at least 10 kilometres away from my military escort through deep twisting tunnels.

Of course, all Insenguardian soldiers are killing machines with their hands and minds.

Yet I think it's fair to say this is not the time for such heroism. Considering I'm surrounded by supernatural foes.

I mean I love witches and warlocks as much as the next Insenguardian but by the Empress it is very annoying when I have to fight them.

I remember I needed to kill one before and usually I just shoot it in the head. But no, the witch didn't have a head to shoot!

Anyway, I have no idea about how to escape.

Calm.

I am an Insenguardian Ambassador. I carry the authority of the God Empress.

I will protect her and she will protect me.

I shall not be able to protect anyone if I die.

Focusing on the situation, I took deep measured breaths.

I pressed my soft hands into the wall.

Damp coldness pulsed through me.

My breath became columns of thick vapour.

The temperature dropped.

In the darkness of the domed chambers with its blood red walls and golden point in the ceiling. I studied for a way out.

In front of me, the Emissary snarled, and the air continued to crackle with magical energy.

The crackles were filled with bright bursts of white, red and pink.

My fear was growing.

I was not going to let it show.

To my left was the snarling creatures that continue to rip themselves out of the wall of the other chamber.

These newer creatures wept a little at the thought of missing the action. Then they licked the bones of my Guard clean.

I couldn't have cared less about my Guards' bones in this moment.

Stretching out my neck, I could see the doorway to the main tunnel and the surface.

A cold pulse washed through me at the thought of the surface.

I thought about going deeper in the tunnels.

A warm sensation washed over me.

I did not know if this was a signal from the Empress, not some demonic trickery from the Emissary.

Yet I knew I had to trust the Empress had a purpose.

The smell of rotting meat and faecal matter filled my nose as the creatures walked closer.

The Emissary raised a hand to them.

They bowed in terror.

Some yelped in fear.

The Emissary took a step closer.

Her earthy perfume starting to become too much for me.

"Are you, you scared yet?"

Her last word slice through the air.

I was taken by the harshness of her words.

Even the creatures seem to cower at her words.

Whatever these things were, they didn't want to be here.

"I am a servant of Insenguard. I know nothing of fear," I attempted.

She playfully stroked my chest and stomach with her long black nails.

I tensed.

She gave a laughter that sounded like logs crackling on a fire.

"Why do this? Your Government wants peace as do I,"

The Emissary stared into my eyes.

I only saw two balls of cold black abyss staring at me.

"Your, your military, military is powerful. Yet I am a member of the Bloody Hand. A Cult you might add. I will destroy you, and ascend to the gave the throne of my Government,"

I was confused.

How would my death help that?

She leaded in closer.

Her damp breath pressing into my ear.

"Your death will spark a war. My Government will burn, and I will replace them,"

"The Empress will ever allow this!"

She pushed away.

Laughing maniacally.

"Your Empress, Empress is not, not here. You are alone,"

My spirit sunk.

She was right.

I was alone.

My Guard dead.

I was a defenceless mortal against

supernatural forces.

I stared into the Emissary's black abysses.

"I might be alone but the Empress is always with me,"

Without thinking I surged forward.
My body sliced through the cold air.
My mind focused on the kill.
I wanted to slaughter her.
I launched punch after punch.
The Emissary dodged each blow.
Her hand flowed rapidly.
Blood covered the floor.
Hissing filled the air.
The blood tried to burn my feet.
They didn't burn.
Her eyes widened.
Those black abysses turned fearful.
The air crackled.
I kicked her to the ground.
Her black dress turned red with blood.
She smiled.
She flicked her hand.
The Creatures charged.
They snarled at me.
I spun around.
Grabbing one creature before I snapped her neck.

More creatures came.
I wished for a gun.
Talons sliced through the air.
I pushed away.
The creatures jumped forward.
Knocking me to the ground.
My back was wet with blood.

My skin felt imaginary flames engulf it.
I wanted to scream.
I needed to scream.
Yet none of this was real.
This was some weird blood magic.
I banished these silly flames from my mind.
The pain was gone.
The talons whipped toward me.
My arms knocked them back.
A talons sliced deep into my arm.
My blood sprayed into the air.
The Creatures laughed in delight.
Staring intensely at the sprays of blood.
I kicked the creatures.
They flew back.
I ripped the head of one creature.
It screamed in agony.
The Creature's blood pooled on the floor.

Without thinking, the other creatures dived on the blood to consume it.

I ran for the door.

An immense stabbing pain came from my back.

I fell to the floor.

I brushed my back with my hands.

I felt something.

Pulling it out, I saw it was one of the Emissary's nails.

I needed to move.

A drop of my blood landed on the floor.

I heard the creature shriek in excitement.

I ran out of the door.

Behind me, I heard the Creatures and the Emissary run after me.

Ready to water the ground with every drop of my blood.

***

My heart raced.

I ran as fast as I could down the tunnel.

The dim light of the endless row of burning torches lit my way deep into the enemy tunnels.

Whatever hope for peace was burnt.

Insenguard could not be peaceful with these creatures.

I kept running.

My feet pounded into the lumpy stone floor.

Shards of rock sliced into my feet.

I prayed my blood wouldn't touch the ground.

I kept running.

My fingers quickly touching the rough sharp edges of the stone on the tunnel walls as I passed.

Hoping for a weapon, I grabbed a shard of rock.

It felt sharp in my hand.

I knew it was useless and reaching the surface was my only hope.

My feet splashed through large puddles of water as I ran.

Water splashed up my legs.

Soaking them.

The bitter coldness of the air steeped into my flesh.

Still my back aced intensely from the wound from the Emissary's nail.

I did have to laugh at myself at the stupidity of it all.

This woman snapped off her own nail to try

and kill me. Who does that?

Equally, I still felt my blood soaking into the soft fabric of my vest.

Soon another drop of blood would land on the ground then the creatures would know my location.

I kept running.

Water continued to splash up my leg.

The smell of disease entered my nose.

An immense crunch echoed in the tunnel.

I felt some flesh fall off my foot.

Maybe I crushed a rat or something?

The cold started to chomp away at my resilience.

My body screamed for rest.

My muscles panted for oxygen.

I needed to breathe.

My heart was thumping in my chest.

In the far distance, I heard tens of footsteps walking this way.

I needed to run.

I turned a corner.

The floor dropped.

I fell into a puddle.

My head whacked into the cold hard stone floor.

My head was cut.

I quickly wiped the blood.

The cut closed.

No blood was spilt.

Freezing cold water covered my clothes.

I shivered.

My toes were numb.

Forcing myself up, I looked around.

I cocked my head.

In front of me, I saw a large golden foundation. Pumping an endless river of blood from a strange dragon mouthpiece to a pool of green jade corpses below.

The entire thing was only a metre high but fear gripped me.

I had read about these fountains.

This culture cut themselves deeply once a week or daily, depending on their fanaticism, to offer their blood god their blood. In exchange, for hope and betterment.

Ridiculous if you ask me.

Action brings around change, not false offerings to false gods.

The footsteps were getting louder.

I have to admit something was telling me I needed divine intervention now.

I hated religion.

But I was going to die.

I remember reading about their blood god and he was described as fair, just and righteousness.

However, some described him as a slaughterer and a slain of men, women and children.

The footsteps got louder.

I needed to run.

My legs shivered.

My limbs were turning numb.

I couldn't run.

Recalling this culture's blood ritual, I looked at the shard of Rock in my hand.

Its long damp sharp brown edges shine in the dim light.

The footsteps were a minute away.

I decided to take the chance.

Staring into the Ruby eyes of the dragon mouthpiece, I sliced deep into my left palm

Rich red blood swelled in my palm.

Tears flooded down my cheeks.

I closed my palm and allowed my thick blood to drip endlessly into the fountain.

The Ruby eyes of the dragon glowed.

I uttered: "With this blood, I command the gods of old and the God of Blood to save me so I may save others and your people,"

Nothing.

The deafening laughs of the creatures echoed in the tunnel.

I heard immense scraps of talons against stone nearby as the reached turned the corner.

I smelt the thick earthy perfume of the Emissary behind me.

A heavy rock smashed into the back of my head.

I felt long talons kiss my flesh.

My world went black.

***

My vision was blurred.

I willed myself to see where I was but I could not.

The back of my head throbbed with wave after wave of immense pain.

I could feel drops of blood run down my back.

My entire body aced from punches, kicks and claw marks.

I focused on my body.

I needed to know how damaged I was.

Best to know how not to fight. The last thing I need is to tear a muscle or something.

I smiled as I remember when I done that before.

I definitely don't want to do that again.

I felt open cuts all over my body. Dripping little bits of blood from the wound.

Even breathing was painful.

That horrid Emissary must have snapped a rip or two.

I needed to escape.

I tried to move.

Pain flooded my entire body.

My muscles screamed in agony.

Tears flooded down my face.

I took a deep breath.

Moving my fingers gently, I managed to feel tight rope digging into my wrists.

I knocked my head back gently.

It whacked into a solid pillar forged from stone.

I was tied up.

In the background, I heard catcalling laughter and screams of delight.

Presumably, the evil creatures were enjoying watching my blood drip onto the ground.

But why didn't they just kill me?

I would like to think with my military history. I was deemed a threat. If not that's just insulting.

My heart quickened at the thought of the darker more twisted possibilities.

My vision started to clear.

I wished it hadn't.

My heart beat turned rapidly.

Sweat poured off my body.

Blood mixed with my sweat.

Tears swelled up in my eyes.

Focusing on every little detail, I saw tens of scaly supernatural creatures with their long talons snarling in front of me.

They looked like they wanted to pounce.

Yet I was tied on a Pyne surrounded by a natural moat of slow swirling blood that floated in the tunnels.

In front of me, a small wooden walkway connected me to the area with the creatures.

The Emissary stood there beaming.

She licked her lips.

Her hand flowed rapidly with blood.

Some of the creatures stared in awe at that so-called delicious blood.

This culture disgusted me, but I wanted to protect it.

I needed to protect the innocent.

I still might not have known why the Empress sent me here, but I know she would want me to save this culture from annihilation.

The Emissary walked gracefully over to me.

Her hand becoming an intense river of blood.

She smiled.

I frowned.

I wanted to scream.

She pointed a long blood flowing nail at me.

All I wanted in this moment was to save my military escort and save this culture from damnation. These cultists would inevitably bring.

She jabbed her bloody nail in my cheek.

I screamed at the pain.

It felt as if a hammer had hit me.

Tears poured out of my eyes.

The Emissary turned to face the hordes of scaly creatures.

They snarled and laughed in delight at the sight of her bloody hand.

She spoke: "Creatures, Creatures of the Bloodied, Bloodied Hand, tonight we sacrifice, sacrifice this Ambassador of pure blood to our Lord. In return, we, we ask, salvation, salvation. Then Creatures, Creatures will not storm the land, land in the name, name of our Lord, Lord,"

The Creatures shrieked in utter excitement at the words and thoughts of sinking their talons into warm juicy flesh.

My heart was pumping as fast as it would go.

The Emissary turned.

I saw her cold black abysses once again.

Then I realised the truth.

I did not care about myself.

I was happy to die.

But I wanted to save my fellow Insenguardians and this culture.

I struggled.

The rope tightened around my wrists.

My fingers were going numb.

The Emissary stood in front of me.

As fast as lightning she sliced deep into my forearms.

Dark blood flooded out of my body.

I went light-headed.

I tried to breathe.

I couldn't.

My skin turned ghostly white.

My skin was soaked in my own blood.

The Creatures shouted with their praise and prays for the Blood God.

The Emissary beamed.

My vision blurred.

Then silence.

I thought I was dead, but I wasn't.

My vision cleared.

My blood returned to my body.

The Emissary's face turned to confusion.

Suddenly, the bubbling blood moat around me churned violently.

Massive blood bubbles exploded.

The moat rose.

The droplets of blood from her sacrifice swirled around me.

Forming immense hurricanes.

The Emissary screamed.

Her bloodied hand was ripped from her by the hurricane.

To my amazement, the hurricane formed the shape of a Bloodied Man.

This figure was immensely tall, and blood dripped from this dark red skin.

He looked at the Creatures and the Emissary.

He roared in rage.

Enormous blood red wings grew from his back.

He charged forward.

It was a massacre.

The Creatures were ripped to shreds.

The Emissary whipped out her blade.

The Angel flicked his wrists.

Her body shattered into hundreds of shards.

The Angel looked at me.

He cocked his head.

He smiled.

Revealing thousands of teeth dripping blood.

He opened his mouth.

He tried to speak.

I thought perhaps he didn't know how to speak.

I mouthed a few words to him.

He understood to use his mouth.

The Angel's claw surged towards me.

My rope bonds were sliced away.

I collapsed to the floor.

He stared at me.

The hard rocky ground dug into my body.

In a bestial, snarling, rageful voice he boomed: "My Master saved you. I am Yours and your Empress'. Save Our People,"

He screamed.

My ears bleed.

An explosion of blood coated the entire chamber.

I wiped my eyes.

The Angel was gone.

Only a small blood red necklace remained with a large ruby inside.

I smiled.

This is why my Empress send me.

She needed allies and a weapon.

She needed me to find it.

Picking up the necklace, I clipped it around my neck.

I felt warm power wash through me.

I had completed my mission to my God

Empress.

    Now I needed to finish my duty and save this culture.

GET YOUR FREE EXCLUSIVE GARRO SHORT STORY HERE!

https://www.subscribepage.com/garrosignup

GET YOUR FREE EXCLUSIVE WINTER SHORT STORY HERE!

https://www.subscribepage.com/wintersignup

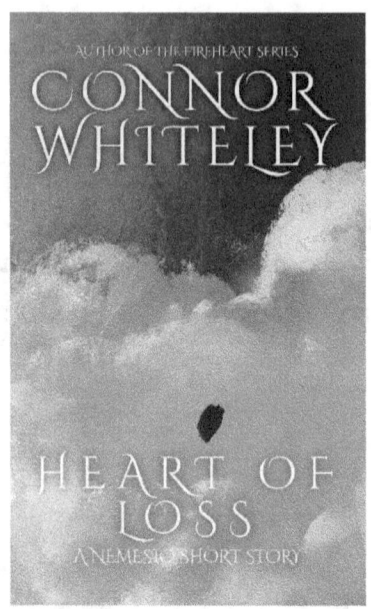

GET YOUR FREE AND EXCLUSIVE SHORT STORY NOW! LEARN ABOUT NEMESIO'S PAST!

https://www.subscribepage.com/fireheart

Thank you for reading.

I hoped you enjoyed it.

If you want a FREE book and keep up to date about new books and project. Then please sign up for my newsletter at
www.connorwhiteley.net/

Have a great day.

About the author:

Connor Whiteley is the author of over 30 books in the sci-fi fantasy, nonfiction psychology and books for writer's genre and he is a Human Branding Speaker and Consultant.

He is a passionate warhammer 40,000 reader, psychology student and author.

Who narrates his own audiobooks and he hosts The Psychology World Podcast.

All whilst studying Psychology at the University of Kent, England.

Also, he was a former Explorer Scout where he gave a speech to the Maltese President in August 2018 and he attended Prince Charles' 70th Birthday Party at Buckingham Palace in May 2018.

Plus, he is a self-confessed coffee lover!

OTHER SHORT STORIES BY CONNOR WHITELEY

Blade of The Emperor

Arbiter's Truth

The Bloodied Rose

Asmodia's Wrath

Heart of A Killer

Emissary of Blood

Computation of Battle

Old One's Wrath

Other books by Connor Whiteley:

The Fireheart Fantasy Series

Heart of Fire

Heart of Lies

More Coming Soon!

The Garro Series- Fantasy/Sci-fi

GARRO: GALAXY'S END

GARRO: RISE OF THE ORDER

GARRO: END TIMES

GARRO: SHORT STORIES

GARRO: COLLECTION

GARRO: HERESY

GARRO: FAITHLESS

GARRO: DESTROYER OF WORLDS

GARRO: COLLECTIONS BOOK 4-6

GARRO: MISTRESS OF BLOOD

GARRO: BEACON OF HOPE

GARRO: END OF DAYS

<u>Winter Series- Fantasy Trilogy Books</u>

WINTER'S COMING

WINTER'S HUNT

WINTER'S REVENGE

WINTER'S DISSENSION

<u>Miscellaneous:</u>

THE ANGEL OF RETURN

THE ANGEL OF FREEDOM

www.ingramcontent.com/pod-product-compliance
Lightning Source LLC
LaVergne TN
LVHW020500080526
838202LV00057B/6064